True Love
and other false models

works of poetry and narrative, from the heroes of *the Multiverse.*

AKASHA TORRES

Mercury Direct

AKASHA TORRES

Mercury Direct
3519 NE 15th Ave #340
Portland, OR 97212
www.mercurydirect.org

Editor: Eva Santiago

ISBN: 0-692-87863-7
ISBN-13: 978-0-692-87863-7

June 3, 2017
Portland, OR

This book is a memoir. It reflects the author's present recollections of experiences over time. These fragments of reality are based on emotional and figurative reflections and are not to be taken as factual accounts.

For the women who were crazy enough to date me.
You knew this was coming.

AKASHA TORRES

PART 1: HUMAN LOVE

INFATUATION

Dear Cupid,

My winged friend, send greetings to your mother.

Congratulations, you've hit your target again. You're a good fellow, Cupid. You've stalked me plenty, taken me out countless times, you shoot blind, I must say, you've outdone yourself this time.

The sweet berry on my lips reminds me of her kiss. How lovely, it is. Her absence tonight makes our morning rendezvous as warm as the sunrise over the eastern sky, and I, would like nothing more than to see her again. To delight thoughts of her, in the moments without her, a fine complement to those moments with her. How well this all works!

Cupid, draw back your bow for the faithful. Fire for the strong-hearted and honest, the noble and true. Contemplate the lovers awaiting you. You were good to me then as you are to me now. And Now.

My heart beats like skipping stones, echoes of thoughts, on the calm ocean of my mind, I ask myself, is this happening? Is the woman there, who kisses me so, and looks at me so, and sees who I am before she knows who I am. Is she the words her eyes speak of? For they speak of beauty and patience, of longing and waiting, of hope and of faith, of God, I awake from this dream. Cupid, am I sleeping?

If I am in my dream, and if here, I awake, let me not be forsaken by the wealth of such dreams. A grand vision of beauty ne'er before touched my heart so. Cupid, you crazy son of Aphrodite, you. Swear upon the River Styx, whether she is my match, or God forbid, my adversary, that you bring beauty to my eyes, and love to my heart, and if for one more wish, I might ask....

Grant her the same.

Honor to the Mother.
Tribute to the Son.
Glory to the God that bends above us all.

CRUSH

I wander along my lonely
street
the silence reveals secret
indiscreet
for all that I chose not
to see
the moonlight casts shadows before my
feet.

Now in my solo fashion
I ponder
upon the root of my true passion
under
the fact that I lack knowledge
of her
and perhaps I must forever
wonder.

But maybe not
methinks I've got
the favor of my gracious
God
for clearly I have been a
nod
for all the right reasons
season's ballade.

And I swear I dare
to say such things
nothing more to lose
but choose to bring
to surface this reality
her heart is calling out
to me.

And I, in all my foolishness
surely, misconstruing this
blind hope and faith, pursuing this
with strength and speed, proceed
I need
to know just who she is
to me.

If I'm in for a broken
heart, so be it, let it take
apart
and rip from my chest
this arrow
dart
so I can breathe again, impart
the passions of my treacherous
heart.

Now with this calculated risk
I decide to be satisfied
with chance, for
its
the only way I can live with
this
for love seeks more than to
exist
and faith awaits a believer's
kiss.

With that, I smile and head for
home
returning to my bed
alone
where awaits astral euphoria
a favorite place
phantasmagoria
and behold her lovely face

Victoria.

PUPPY LOVE

we were kids then
only seventeen
guessing at love
stumbling through life.

the world was an adventure
and we weren't afraid
we'd live forever
or so we thought.

i called her
crying
my first love
had
broken
my heart.

she called me
crying
her second
love
wasn't
me and

yet it wasn't so complicated
she still crawled
into my bed
my arms
whenever it rained
too hard.

she taught me how to
roll
a joint.

i taught her how to
drive
and she did.

ninety miles an
hour in a
thirty-five
zone

whiskey on her
breath

it wasn't my
fault.

one last phone call.

silence.

waiting for the other
to say

three words
that never came.

her mom said
she would come to
see me during
spring break.

i
was going to
tell her then.

i
was going to show
her

my run down
studio, no
job or school
just hustle.

i
had it all
figured out.

we couldn't be
lovers, but i'd be
her best

friend.

well
fuck.

there's no future
when you're
seventeen.

just one
glorious moment in which
you live
forever.

but now i know better
because i've grown
up and
she's still

seventeen.

CURIOSITY

Tis sweet defeat to love, says Lo
Answers Vick, thine sugar is rancid
Am I then dunce, asks I, or no
For defeat cannot be tasted.

Vick, he laughs at I, and bends
Young knave, if defeat is thine candy
Then retire thine tongue, or now, perpend
Thou death is thy life's own fancy.

Lo, she fronts, thou fear the child
With thine zany words, I shrift
Love is unsure, unsafe, and wild
Yet without such Love, is one adrift.

The two undergo such testy balk
While I abhor their argued tenses
For Love is silent, and fools do talk
Neither doth Love to sit on fences.

And still my mind doth will to capture
Such honest and absolute, thus rapture.

ADDICTION

Although food for the spirit
and pleasure for the body
for the broken soul
love is a deadly addiction

a
methamphetamine

for me
more like
manic-depression.

Natural
disorder of the
mind, wise folly
of the
heart
romantic
Russian roulette
and yet

promising of euphoric
episodes of lofty
philosophies

higher consciousness
cosmic bliss
then this
is followed

by
orgasmic truths
exploding synapses
because
love

dwelleth in the highest
of skies, and
as high as
one flies
is as low as one's
doom

and
as the weight of
addiction finds
gravity, racing
toward
the earth at a
skull
splitting
velocity

the manic-depressive prepares his
noose

and love
is
replaced
as
driver
to be
driven
by this
demon

fear

and plunges
into
the brackish lake
of
heartache.

this is your
heart on
love.

But then
like a fresh
line
of cocaine

I awaken
from my
darkest hour

to once again
find
magnificent wings

upon my
shoulder blades

and the
angelic smile
of my lover
in the slowly
passing clouds

and as the
pendulum
swings
violently
toward the
opposite extreme

I fight
for stillness
and silence
and cry out
to my
God.

It is here
in my sober
mind that
I find

love without excess
requires
the discipline of
balance

and each night
as I watch her
loveliness drift
away into dreams
like
the majestic
setting sun over

the ocean's horizon
I realize

that
love is a
drug
only
for the volatile
heart

but for the
strong-willed
and courageous

love is a state
of being

that
must
be maintained
through constant
vigilance.

Only then
when the brave
lion embraces their
tender heart
can

true
love

be experienced
in its most natural
brilliance.

Alas, love is a riddle that can only be
solved by the
heart.

FANTASY BOND

The lover in my dreams
seem to remember me
each time I find
myself in my mind.

My body so still
all of my will
perfectly channeled
and filled.

With the woman in outer
space, without a face, yet
her hands know even my
darkest place, erase.

Everything you know
about reality, finding truth
humanity, me and my
love, we are insanity.

And the laws of physics
don't apply, forget it, and
fly, the sky is how we get
high, and I, am lost as she.

Is found, her words
without sound, take me
deeper, profound, unground
and unbound, I could live.

Here forever, but never, for
sound. My snowflake heart
death is this world, ripping
me, tearing me, from my.

Dream girl. Each time I
hear the knock at my
door, my heart, again
pierced, the pain, anger.

Fierce. And I fight to remain
still, all of my will, all my

strength, to keep me
from tossing and turning.

My rage in chest, burning
still trying my best, yearning
I guess my dreams fade into
nothingness. The alarming.

Moment in which I awoke
like the stroke of a sword
like the wrath of my lord
humbling, to the floor, tumbling.

And once more, I cry out
implore, for the feeling of
her hands, slipping from mine
disappearing with time, never.

Again to be mine, for this crime
of mine, love, I am doing my time.
So how could I write the words
"happily ever after," when I've.

Sought after laughter, and
morning brings disaster
and my master remains
silent, for the gods made of.

Plaster, they scream for me
master, for they fear I am
chaster, and my lover
they grasp her, so tightly.

I ask her, but she fades away
with the sound of her laughter.
And I seem to chase, the lover
without face. The things this brings.

The fairies without wings, the
silent lark sings of fear as it
clings to one powerful ring
to wear, oh to bear, this burden.

I swear, is the knight without

heart, into the dragon's lair.
And as I lay there, still the
pounding my door, as my.

Heart's tore apart to face
reality's sharp dagger of
truth, gather the strength of
my youth, and once again bid.

Farewell
to my dream lover
you.

ATTACHMENT

There in the deepest
recesses of my
mind

subconscious dark
corners, a
child hides.

She works my
ego with
remote

devices, hydraulic
arms and
sacrifices.

Tricks and
smoke, drugs
fear, addiction.

She's befriended
demons
has their
affection.

A void
avoided
a mom
not dad.

She seeks
a love she's never
had.

Mastered silence and
stillness
but knows not
peace.

She often pretends
to be deceased.

A ghost, she
haunts the corridors
of my mind

locks more doors
to find

a mommy
outside.

It's been taken
again, her lifeline
friend, she'll
die for sure

this is the end.

But she doesn't
see, this is
why they leave.

Why won't she stop
crying?
shut the fuck up

please?!

Shut up! Just shut the fuck up!

And go away!

NO ONE LOVES YOU
NO ONE EVER WILL

NO ONE EVER LOVED ME
YOU STUPID LITTLE

GIRL.

SURVIVAL

A nameless ocean
unspoken notions
anticipation for the deep
if it means rest
in peace.

Without breath
or need
or delusion
or me.

In a world
forsaken
for a moment
taken for granted
mistaken.

The ocean floor
promises my
heart
nothing
untrue.

Shall I inhale
to see the
deep or will
I spend the
rest of my time

Treading
?

VICIOUS CYCLES

From the depths
Of my
Soul

I scream
For her.
She has

Taken
Her lips
And left me

With this
Memory of her
Kiss.

She has
Chastened
Her body

From me.
For him.

She called
Him
Perfection.

It must be true
For I
Lay alone

And he
Next to
You.

His hands
To caress
And
Adore

Her beautiful flesh
While I

Remember

The sound of
Her breath
The scent of
Her
Breasts

The taste of
Her
Depths

For him.

All of she
Is for
Him.

And he for
you.

What the hell is wrong
with you?

Tell me
What is valued greater
Than
Love
?

You claim
Great faith
Then forfeit
Because

You're addicted
To
Chains

I'm addicted
To
Pain

Hence, I'm still

In love
And I'll say it
Again.

How could I
Stand to be
Your friend?

A casual talk
Cold embrace

They're lies
I see it in
Your face

Passion leaks
Through your
Eyes, deep

Longing they
Imply, that your
Life without

Me, is one
Big
Fat
Lie.

You say that
I'm wrong,
And call me

Misguided, dismiss
Me today, you'll
Call me on

Friday.

And we'll
Play make pretend
Until I

Say when.

Mercy, my love.
I'll take what
You'll give, I'll

Make it enough
For five out ten
Is better than

Two as
No woman alive
Is better than

You. Baby, what
Can I do
?

I suffer for
You.
And as

All
My anger and
All my
Pain

Tempt me to
Push you away

I
Sway.

For your melodic
Touch

Melting
Me.

Stirring my
Heart with the
Tips of your
Fingers.

Once again
You find a

Home

In my arms
I know it
Hurts

But I mean you
No harm. Though
I will never

Understand why you
Choose him over
Me, I see

We have
Sinned

[incomprehensible whisper]

Forgive me
Forgive
Us.

As this
Heartache lingers.

God
I see
It now.

The
Ring on her

Finger.

THE EVIL QUEEN

Her eyes speak lies
her touch, the truth
this justifies
her sunken tooth.

Scorpio sun
Plutonian shore
civil war begun
for I love her more.

She loves my masochism
laughs at core wounds
inspires violence
she controls my doom.

She brings the pain
I think I deserve
vicious cycles, insane
belief systems, merged.

My heart in her hands
in her grip, tightening
I pray, please understand
she says, "obey me."

A mind fuck to hell
death trail, nostalgic journey
slow suicide, comfortable cell
a sacrifice, unworthy.

Many times, I did run on
down that sacred road red
but the Evil Queen is no demon
she's my shadow, reflected

"I will appear, as I should
in every woman you love."
So far, her word has been good
shattered hearts, enough.

Magick mirror, truth bring
to the surface what is lying

in shadow, Snow White, sleeping.
The Masculine is I, Prince Charming.

(to be continued....)

PART 2: DIVINE LOVE

VERONICA

I would give up everything
for a Love that would
illuminate

the dark sub-chambers
of my heart
unexplored

with a flaming torch
in an ancient
tomb, I

discovered
me with
you.

You
are a single match
tossed carelessly

upon the
dying embers of my
dormant

soul
awakening me, now
I

am alive
I
am an inextinguishable

forest
fire of
passion

my flames
licking at the
heavens for a

taste of
you

again.

You
are the
gravity, holding

me to this
world,
while my fantastic

flights of
fiction tempt me to
escape

the
reality of your
absence

of the
places we
consecrated

with our
sacred
Love

now
haunted
by the

ghosts
of
your fingertips

across my
skin.
You

are the angel
in my
dreams, feeding

my heart the
beauty

it needs to

face my own
monsters
the person in the

mirror
I saw myself in your
eyes, I saw you in the

higher skies
and when you
walked out

of my life
I knew
that fighting

for you
didn't mean locking
you in and

begging
at your feet
it meant

falling
to my knees
and watching

you
leave.
Because

I saw
magnificent wings
fixed upon your

shoulder blades
and
I wanted to

see you
fly

in that

sky
much more than
I

wanted
you to
be mine.

Now you are
gone, and I
can never be

the same, you have
changed
me

like a
newborn
baby

Christian
my faith
has been

renewed
I
have the strength of

ten men or
more
in the

core of my
soul, in the
beat of

my
heart.
I

beheld your inner
Truth for only

three seconds

and
I
was

transformed.

TWIN FLAME?

The present question is quite perplexing, a foreign
phenomenon, and matter pressing, upon my
heart, my mind, progressing, forward, stressing
this mystery must be explored.

The subject, female, physically fit, brown eyes and skin
full set of lips, her hips, and waist, pretty face
embrace, the magic on her finger tips.
How might one measure the effect of this?

Her gaze strikes intentionally, the crux of me
especially, while the lips touch
delicately, an oxytocin-soaked brain
chemistry, chain reactions to her kiss, sexual
attraction, but its
so much more than this.

In the act of making love, I see, under her
freckled skin, within, reflection of me, as
the hands of time, halted on my
heart's command, a bending silver spoon, I
witnessed impossibility.

The clock ceased its tick, and gravity, it had no effect
here I pause to reflect
on the subject, the flickering candle of our soul, poetry
no, one must be logical in saying
that it unifies theory.

The reality of eternity was suddenly conceived
certainly, my body affirms this
pleasure, well received, an epiphany
of affinity, measuring infinity, now perceive
my heart
transformation thus achieved.

The gravity between us convicted me
of my true identity, in a single moment, aesthetically, as
if we had loved before, hypothetically
this would explain the intensity

by which we were
united.

The subject bears a magnetic field, opposite in polarity
to mine, and despite the
ever-changing labyrinth of her
mind
the energy is constant
transcending time.

I am certain the subject is not
conscious of the impossible symmetry of this
paradox, which is, our very soul, leading to the
hypothesis, the heightened sense of
timelessness. I
know

That under her precious flesh, the energy abreast, is one
half of me, yet whole in itself, is current with flow
source frequency, light, allowing for errors
she is my twin
could this be
right?

FEED THE WORLD

I could feed the whole world on the crumbs of her Love.

Listen.

A single word upon her lips expresses a compassion so great
    it could heal the great plaque of the undead
      suffering the silent horrors of a soul holocaust.

The sleeping and dying in the gutters of hopelessness.
    Women, children, men, clutching their bellies, starving for Truth
    come one, come all, gather around
    for I have heard her voice today.

And there is enough Love to feed the world.

The Light in her eyes is bright enough to pierce the densest
    of darkness, the most terrible and oppressive of fears
      my childhood demons tremble in her presence.

As she breaks through the blackest and heaviest of storms
    she has the power of a thousand stars, like nuclear fusion in her core
      too hot to approach, she is cool to the touch, and unaware of her.

Prism, breaking down heavenly Light for our infantile human eyes
    so come, you who are afraid and down trodden
      you who weep and gnash your teeth in the shadows.

Open your third eye, for I
    have seen her face today, and there is
    enough Light to feed the world.

Her beauty is unsurpassed by anything in nature
    for so natural is she, and the nature of beautiful
      things are pale reflections of her truth.

O flowers, O mountains, O sunsets, O cosmic miracles in
    the infrared false color, behold, the essence of
      your Maker, settles on the surface of her skin.

Penetrating to the depths of her very soul, her beauty transmutes
    the most hideous of sights, so I invite you
    dear ugly, dear inadequate, dear loser, dear liar.

Dear pathetic pieces of shit, come, for I have felt her heartbeat
    today, and its beauty is sufficient
    to uncover your own.

Her potential is a thousand forests in a single tiny seed, the
    spark of a million big bangs, stretch
    expand, to all infinite parallel universes.

This dimension cannot contain her, and when she
    harnesses this power, there will be no more
    suffering, no more sorrow, a utopian planet of.

Barefoot hippies, there will be no tears in Heaven and no religion
    created by man could worship the Divine
    within her, like I will, when she sets herself.

Free, so come, ye of little faith, come satanist, come terrorist, come
    hearts full of hate, for I have
    peered into her eyes today, and.

There are enough miracles to change the world.

I could feed the whole world on the crumbs of her Love.

And if I never see her again, it will have been enough.
    I could still live forever on the prana of a
    timeless memory, breathing in a Love.

So deep, so alive, an everlasting fountain of the Sacred Heart
    of Jesus Christ. And all the blind optimism of my
    Sagittarian aim could not have imagined a Love.

So great, so amazing, so transcendent of any human
    experience ever recorded in my breathless heart.

So, what happens next is irrelevant. All hopes and.

Dreams, all pending fantasies, now bow at the knees to this
    Divine reality: I am satisfied with only the
    Crumbs of her Love, for with it.

I can feed the whole world. It's much more than enough.

ETERNAL CHILD

Dear Ella,

I've been sitting here with this box of bones, and sticks, fairy dust, and glue, trying to detach my shadow from thoughts of you.

Remember when I said I had run away from home, from you, that I never wanted a mother, another, nor lover? No, none was true.

I think the curse is broken now, the dark ones have gone home, their voices, like choices, and noises, well, I have been alone.

Cupid did visit, that wise little Cricket, in attendance, a few angels, and earth spirits, too, our mutual friends, these adventures with you.

I lost some baby teeth today, chasing the fairies away, I'd never say never, and Round Knights know better, still, even grown ups must play.

Our imaginary places, inter-dimensional spaces, no faces of plastic, and phases, no more tragic than if we should forget magic!

Now you have flown to that warm window, my home, my Love, not as simple, I know, it is time to let go, a button for a thimble?

The children are asleep now, and we too grow up. Do not fear, my darling dear, see here, two of cups, filled up.

Maybe I will be grown one day, and maybe you will be my wife, or maybe this is a child's dream, and this love, for another life.

To pass the test, and earn the badge, I cross my chest, like a good ol' Sadge, at quest, I promise, we shall come out of this, reborn.

Like the flaming bird, Ella, in the night skies of the crying eyes of children, surprised of our Fae allies, and boom, realize!

Now farewell, goodbye, boys can cry, and girls can fly, and I, will miss you, mommy, goodbye, I mean, my beautiful friend, my best fairy.

Til the end,
Just Imaginary

VERONICA, PART 2

This message is for a woman who no longer exists. Please, if you see her, please tell her this.

I still see your face whenever I close my eyes. I still feel you in my chest, on the left side, I, am not sure which dimension I am living, a pocket universe, a make-pretend city. But the mirage in the rearview appears even nearer, as if the farther I drive, the crystal get clearer, unconscious acts, I see, through mirrors, a tell-tale tarot, the dream just gets weirder.

I'm not sure how you managed the escape speed, defying laws, like gravity, still just a theory, because our best times, were all in my mind, colorblind, my twisted head, a mathematic equation, experimenting in bed, and yet, imagination, Einstein once said, was more important, red, and so I fed the lies, fantasized, the truth despised. These delusions, reclusions, some cosmic confusion, and I'm not sure if you were ever real.

I think you have somehow become numb to me, the pain in cheek, with doublespeak, novocain, somas, and TCH, I can't say how this has come to be, but whatever it is you are taking, please, save some for me. I don't want to feel this anymore.

Except I do, a fool, for Love is true, and here, the proof, you, dear, have summoned my fear, from bottomless hell, you, some evil spell, no, curse, so much worse, and more urgently, impertinently, don't touch me, I'm ugly, and certainly unworthy, neglected, rejected, this open wound, infected. Sought medicine, relief, clear the grief, congested, and terror, suspected, of sabotage, error, corrected.

Then introspected, healed and well-rested, honorable, respected, my whole world affected, now this Love, interconnected.

Forgive me, I have fallen short of my Truth, and likewise, you, are human, too.

This mess we made, an interfusion, our best would fade, sought absolution, and substitutions, made so many resolutions, still children, we are, in the grand scheme, stars, team evolution, this holy theme, Love revolution, and Truth seen, high resolution, it's time, supreme, to let go of this dream.

So to my queen, from her dear pawn, please listen, whether fiction, or non, imaginary friend, or foe, such woe, forgiven, and escaped from these prisons, attachment, like chains, addictions, like pain, incisions, and pages blood-written, and turned, dark towers, burned, new lessons, learned, and imprinting, angels singing, here I call in a New Beginning.

I Love you. I always will. Be happy, my Love. Be well.

SOMETIMES

Sometimes True Love is the silence between text messages, when she's angry and wants to clear her head before responding.

Sometimes it's staying up all night trying to see her point of view, when you're just as angry as she is.

Sometimes True Love is creating a safe space for her to come home to, after she's friendzoned you about a thousand times.

Sometimes it's facing your Self alone, healing your wounds, and becoming the person you are meant to be.

Sometimes True Love is releasing your expectations, letting go of naive dreams, tainted self-images, and egoic platforms.

Sometimes it's walking a path alone, because once you have tasted True Love, anything else is but a poisoned apple.

Sometimes True Love is wishing for her happiness in the arms of another, knowing that the other does not Love her.

Sometimes it's gathering all the strength in your being to restrain your tongue when angry, to sit when you'd rather stand.

Sometimes True Love is granting forgiveness before the apology, and understanding before the explanations.

Sometimes it's open-hearted listening as she tells her tales, heart adventures with unworthy suitors.

Sometimes True Love is realizing that without friendship, there is no foundation upon which to build a life-long partnership.

Sometimes it means finding the light of faith in dark places, strength within the struggle, and medicine in the sickness.

Sometimes True Love is knowing that you'll be okay, no matter how it turns out, because you're a goddamn soldier, and this, too, is perfect.

Sometimes True Love is nothing more than being there for a friend, again, and again, and again.

PRINCE CHARMING

(Continued…)

Fear not, children, hallow
 lost in these enchanted realms
 the Evil Queen is just a shadow
 master of the ego self.

Disarm the Evil Queen
 with pure, steady, True Love.
 Awareness, the kiss, awake dream
 will break the curse, trust.

When the repressed feminine is loved, right
 for the brilliant survivor that she is
 then awakens your Snow White.
 If she is your equal, you are a Prince.

However, I must warn, only
 True Love breaks the spell.
 Attachment springs her trap, see
 worthlessness, impotence, well.

Face your Self before you attempt
 to approach the Evil Queen
 lies, lullabies, poison apples tempt
 the drug for which you fiend.

Achieve first royalty of heart
 train with honor, valor, integrity
 You are the lion in the strength card
 Tamed through patient empathy.

Only True Love breaks the curse
 if you were mistaken, taken victim
 and you do not Love her, worse
 hate her, you've been tricked, run!

The Evil Queen, this dirge she sings
 as the King was once a monster
 like Maleficent, broken wings
 give her lots of time to ponder.

Give her space to feel
    the freedom to soar
    the medicine to heal
    and unlock your doors.

She will come, senses heightened
    like the phoenix, rising
    she will blow your mind, enlightened
    Snow White, a light, blinding.

Keep your balance, brave, open
    heart, vulnerable and safe
    let the dark, through love, be spoken
    patience with, the path be paved.

You are her protection, guard
    her well, introspection, and Truth
    discipline led by the heart
    teach, be taught, parent to youth.

The darkness cannot be cast out
    without first descent of mind
    carry your Light, humble, proud
    judgment fails, each time.

Remember your code of honor
    banner of Love upon your chest
    bend to glory, kneel, proper
    God, Goddess, achieve the rest.

Then, O knight of valor
    I dub thee, rise, the rapture
    this quest of Divine matter
    yours, the happily every after.

THE SLEEPING GODDESS

My golden heart rests
    on the altar of the sleeping goddess.

I tend it with care, renewing
    offerings, like devotion and incense.

As my goddess, she stirs
    talks of dreams and of faith

I vow to protect her sacred space.

While others chase illusion
    condemning my reverence

I remain at her altar
    in Love and in presence.

SLUSHED DEDICATION

For a woman who shall remain unnamed here
at her request.

For the brave soul who volunteered to serve as a reflection
of my shadow.

For the Evil Queen
of Hearts
For Cleopatra VII.

For the one who taught me how to
Love my Self
by refusing me
Love.

For the woman whose heart was
stolen and destroyed
time and again
as I watched
with my idle sword
watched
with my impotent wand
watched
as she swallowed the blue
pill
and tossed me into
the abyss
of
unconsciousness
and forgot
that I
was
a person
she cherished.

For forgiveness
and compassion.

For True Love.

For my imaginary friend
from way back when.

For the collective Feminine.

I pray thee
sleepy goddess

Awaken!

PART 3: THE LOVE PAPERS
the ascension of Nikola Woolf

After accidentally creating a virus that catalyzes rapid evolution of the human genome, Dr. Nikola Woolf is metamorphosing into a fifth dimensional being, capable of traveling to parallel universes. However, the complications of the experiment, a mission to define and "cure" True Love, may cost her life. While involuntarily traveling the Multiverse, Nikola learns that the extinction of humanity is imminent in many worlds. Will Dr. Woolf survive her own ascension, can she save the human race, and what will she do about her unwanted True Love?

FORWARD

by Dr. Jake O'Connor:

Dr. Nikola Woolf is a celebrated geneticist, New York Times Bestselling author of *ADD Equals Genius*, *The Psychic Gene*, and *Evolution of the Mind*; co-creator of the gene therapy cure for ADD/HD; graduate of Stanford University; and outspoken proponent of the controversial Aquatic Ape Theory.

The following pages is a compilation of the found documents of Dr. Nikola Woolf and Kelly Perez. They are in the form of letters, raw data, journal entries, text message threads, and narratives.

The mysteries surrounding their disappearance has earned the attention of the FBI, CIA, and several covert international agencies.

The State of California has released death certificates, deeming the cause of death "lost at sea." However, the vessel, a thirty-foot sailing yacht, was confiscated by a government agent off the coast of Aogashima, Japan. After a thorough search of land, sea, and air, the Marine officer charged with overseeing the task has confirmed that no bodies were found. The official story was later revised. I am convinced they are alive.

I have reviewed Dr. Woolf's fascinating research, and risked everything to protect her secret. A data report has been compiled and sent to approximately six hundred laboratories. All I have left are these pages, *The Love Papers*, as Dr. Woolf so affectionally called it.

CHAPTER 1

Nikola Woolf
The Letterhead

The Woolf Institute
321 Silent Way
Santa Barbara, CA 93101

2022 DEC 18

Dear Lisa,

I apologize for keeping this from you. My intention was your protection. I have set a series of events into motion and it cannot be undone. My time is limited. I have not written a formal paper, mostly because the results are yet inconclusive. By the time I'm able to conceive of this phenomena, this dimension will no longer sustain me. Enclosed, you will find the raw data, journal entries, and my final will and testament. The narrative by Kelly Perez is here, too.

I need you to publish this, but only in paperback. Please have Caleb do this for me. There can be no electronic records of this book, do you understand? They are to be distributed by hand to:

Dr. Jacob O'Connor of Kona, HI
Dr. John Everett of Riverside, CA
Major Timothy F. Johnson, USMC. The book is for his son, Geoffrey, who will one day pass it down to his first daughter.

There will be more.

NW

P.S. Thank you for being my best friend. I love you.

The Woolf Institute
321 Silent Way
Santa Barbara, CA 93101

2022 AUG 04

TO THE KEEPER OF THESE PAGES:

Please protect this record. They fear the uprising of the human race.

The Woolf Institute is a government funded lab. We study child neurology and specialize in creating genetic treatments which assist the regulatory brain function of the rapidly evolving mind, while supporting, rather than blocking, the natural progression of evolution.

We work with child prodigies. All children falling in the gifted range, outside the bell curve on both sides, are genius. They are remarkably more evolved than the norm.

When a prodigy is deemed mentally-ill and medicated, their brilliance punished for the sake of an academic standard, for conformity, the child's self-esteem suffers, unique talents snuffed.

The effects of academic standardization are intended to arrest the development of gifted humans. There exists a network of social systems, an agenda to freeze human evolution. This is quite apparent, I know. More of this later.

These children should study, tuition free, at special education academies. They are our future. We have a moral duty to see that they are psychologically well nourished.

Lisa and Luke, my colleagues, believe in my work. That is, until the day I revealed my intention to move forward with the Love Papers. What they didn't know is that the project was already in progress.

Nikola Woolf

Luke stood above me, his messy blonde hair falling over his pink face. "I cannot let you do this." Luke formerly studied psychology. His dissertation and dissent of psychiatric practices intrigued me enough to secure a tuition grant. After a two-year internship, and at twenty-three years old, he became the youngest neurologist in the nation.

Lisa was pacing the rectangle-shaped room, her black curls bouncing with each step. She shook her head, lips pursed.

Her angst was a consolation to me. I would not have to concern myself with things that Lisa took upon herself. She wouldn't realize how much I depended on her, for she was focused on the secrets I kept.

As a physiologist, her true desire was to practice in an emergency room. She longed for chaos, but feared it with equal passion. She has sworn dedication to my cause, but the real reason she stayed at the institute, is fear.

Lisa paused, her lips pursed with profane intentions, and shifted toward Luke. "Watch your mouth, Skywalker. You need to reason with her."

Luke threw his arms up. "But she's not being reasonable."

Lisa nodded, trying to control her anger. "All the more reason you should be."

I know what you're thinking. How am I aware of Lisa's thoughts or intentions? Of course, she's my best friend. It's more than that. These developments, or gifts, are new to me. You will see.

A silent moment came upon us. I waited for Luke to gather himself. Finally, he sat at the table. He took a deep breath.

"Nikola," his green eyes were focused on me. "I respect you. We've done amazing things here. I see that we have the potential to do much more. But the truth is that if you decide to study love, all our progress will mean nothing. The truth is that love can't be studied, Nikola."

I heard his words, and I felt his passionate fear. He was being logical, as expected. However, he was missing the very thing I was searching for. It was this lack of understanding that perpetuated such meaninglessness.

Luke represented the old paradigm, the path humanity had been on for some thousands of years now, one that would lead to further destruction and the extinction of the human race. Unless.

Luke stood and waved his finger in my face. "You want to know what love is? I'll tell you. It's dopamine, serotonin, and oxytocin. That's it."

Lisa stepped closer, her volume increasing as she struggled to gain control. She didn't understand everything she was feeling yet. She trusted her emotions. "That's not love, you idiot. It's the chemical reaction to infatuation. You're such a dude."

Luke placed his hands on the table and leaned in toward Lisa. "It's the only thing that can be measured. And it's already been done. Study closed. And if you're suggesting that my gender can more readily perceive the obvious truth, well, you're absolutely correct." He turned his back. "Dr.

Brain?"

A giant cartoon mouse wearing a white lab coat, appeared beside him. Dr. Brain was Luke's holographic assistant. "Yes, Dr. Novick?"

Luke faced the hologram. "Your image is breaking up."

It wasn't true. Luke was making an excuse to shut the system down. You see, we were being monitored via the Wall Interface Computer. Every event in the facility was recorded and considered property of the US government. There were ways around the system. Luke knew them, too.

"Dr. Brain," Luke said, "restart the system immediately." He whirled around. I felt his focus, like a laser beam, fixed on my head.

The computer voice echoed throughout the room. "System shutting down. Goodbye."

Luke placed his hands at his hips. "I want to know what you've been doing after hours."

Lisa scoffed, but under the surface, she wanted to know, too.

I had to tell them at some point. I had put their careers in jeopardy, perhaps even their lives. Soon, the revelation would come. But then was not the time. Disclosure would hinder my progress. I had to stall.

I met his eyes. "The logs are public, Luke."

He crossed his arms and tilted his head. "I've seen the logs. They account for the supplies, but not for the time. Moreover, I've detected a-"

"Watch your step, Skywalker," Lisa said. "Don't forget who signs your paycheck. This is her lab."

"It's my career," Luke said. "Our careers. Or have we forgotten that we're scientists, not giddy high school girls?"

Lisa pointed at Luke's face, fighting the urge to slap it. "Insult Nikola one more time, and you are done."

I sat up and exhaled. I would fix this. But not now. Besides, the computer would restart in eleven and a half seconds. "Alright, let's just call it a day. Okay? We all need to think things through." I adjusted my glasses and met Luke's eyes.

Luke pressed his lips and took a deep breath before speaking. "Nikola, I love you. I love working with you. Your mind is beautiful. I love how you go straight to the most radical idea, and persist until you uncover some fascinating truth." He pressed his thumb and index finger together. "It's what makes you so brilliant. But this time, you're going too far. And I beg you to reconsider. Please, Nikola." His mouth hung open for a moment. His green eyes moved sideways, then back to me. "I don't want to have to leave you."

I lowered my gaze. I had expected resistance from Luke. I didn't predict it would hurt.

"You fucking prick," Lisa said, as he walked out. "I can't believe he just threatened you."

The computer voice sounded, on time. "System commence. Welcome, Doctors."

Alone with Lisa, I could feel the conflict inside her more clearly. She wanted to protect me and my project, but she was also hurt that I had not shared it with her. She wanted to know, but she was too afraid to ask.

It's not that I didn't trust her. Ignorance was her protection. The CIA would label her a terrorist and would not give her the right to remain silent.

Lisa dropped into the chair beside me. "Hey. Fuck him. He's just a kid."

I met her brown eyes, unsure, afraid. I exhaled. "He's a genius, Lisa."

Annoyed, Lisa glanced down at her watch. It was happy hour, and her kids were at her parents. She wants to get a drink, I thought.

Lisa slammed her palm onto the table. "We should get a drink."

The Woolf Institute

321 Silent Way
Santa Barbara, CA 93101

QUESTION:

The purpose of this study is to define and quantify true love in contrast to false models; to record its effect on the human toroidal field; to establish a set of universal laws upon which love operates; and to create a gene-therapy cure for such disorder.

The question of love has been evaded by modern science for lack of definition, perspective, and technology. It is here that I perceive a mystery more intriguing than mere romance. The world hungers for this elusive substance. I find myself compelled, perhaps even guided, to explore these ideas, like shadows in the mirrors of the labyrinth in my mind.

I feel a deadly current here, a riptide, threatening to drag me out into the open sea of nothingness, a place I'm sure exists. I'm terrified, but I won't resist.

The human genome and all its information will fail to define the meaning of life if, within it, we cannot understand love.

2022 FEB 27

I fear for my sanity. I often awaken in the dead of night in a cold sweat, with the fright of otherworldly danger, looming ahead. These places in my mind become realities short of time. No, surely, just dreams.

The thing that terrifies me most is my own awareness and connection to, the totality of energy in all the cosmos, far beyond my own existence, yet one with all. The paradoxes unfold like the thousand-petaled lotus, from out of the darkness, into the light.

2022 MAR 2

Today should be like any other day. The sun rises in the East as life awakens. Yellow light pierces the morning shadows, through the blinds. The rays illuminate the dust in the room.

I am still at my desk.

There are no outward indications of the inner transformation. There is nothing that can be measured to account for this phenomenon. Yet. I am still observing.

Could the scientific mind settle for abstract philosophies in self-defeat? There are paths, lit by strings of ideas. I feel, rather than think, that there is a method awaiting its discovery.

2022 MAR 5

Love had always been foreign to me. My previous consideration defined love as a psychological disorder, a coping mechanism, a chemical satisfaction, the attachment to objects outside of oneself for comfort and momentary happiness. Love was but a fairytale for those who required fiction to provide a sense of purpose to an otherwise meaningless existence.

Emptiness was the reality upon which I built my identity, the "truth." The void, the chasm of entropy, the vacuum of spacetime was, to me, the womb of all.

Today, those spaces are filling in with impossible ratios, and precise symmetry. My own capacity for knowledge is too small for such volumes, and yet I find myself beyond... myself.

My very existence is expanding by the moment, my conscious mind reforming with every channeled thought. There seems to be an ever-present, omnipotent intelligence, the superconscious, whose thoughts are algorithms, the codes of life, which is the very material of life, both physical and etheric.

I dare not postulate religious fantasies, and yet, I have succumbed to a force much greater than myself.

I am not the same. Everything I have ever known is wrong. How could I present myself, a know-nothing scientist, to a world that depends on me for absolute truth?

CHAPTER 2

Kelly Perez
A Mother Fucking Story

March 11, 2014

While everyone waited for me to get over her, my love kept getting stronger.

Months went by since I left everything behind and moved to Los Angeles, to her home city. Her territory. Her friends and family. Her job, her school. Her everything.

I had nothing.

I knew that she was walking away. I heard it in her voice. I had nightmares about it.

I was the one who told her to follow her heart. I just hoped it would lead her to me.

In her absence my love increases. There's no proof to support any hopes that she'll come back. Yet I'm falling harder everyday. This makes no sense.

Love is for idiots.

It wasn't love. How could it have been?

The next logical (and paradoxically illogical) idea that came is that there was nothing it could be except love. Yeah, of course. Why else would I find myself completely alone and disoriented in a new city while spiraling downward and talking to imaginary people?

True Love.

Hi. My name is Kelly.

I have no idea why anyone would call me an expert on love, but someone did. Then I got asked to write a paper about love. Like, with a thesis and everything? Okay. Let's get all academic and shit.

No ways, dude. I don't do essays or theses, or any of it. I dropped out of college. I studied English Lit on my Kindle, and Filmography on my Sony. I don't have time for the other stuff. I mean, I like to read, but only if I get to pick the book.

You know what's better than a boring essay? A mother fucking story.

This is a story about an archetype, a famous pair of lovers, living their tales of romance and tragedy, nameless within the collective mind. Or, in literature as Pyramus and Thisbe, Romeo and Juliet. In the Hindu religion, they are Shiva and Shakti. In Egypt, they are Osiris and Isis. In gnostic Christianity, they are Jesus and Magdalene.

These epic stories, however, were misunderstood, misinterpreted, and straight up manipulated. Why?

Unless you're ready to get into a serious Ancient Aliens discussion, which may or may not lead to ET contact of the fifth kind, well. Let's not go there. The point is, I'm about to set it right.

Here I present a modern version of the ancient archetype called Twin Flames.

By the way, this is all fiction. None of this really happened. I've been dreaming about this woman, you see. Yeah.

'Twas a midsummer night's dream....

I got kicked out of the bar for being drunk. What the hell is alcohol supposed to do, make me shit rainbows?

I didn't agree with the bouncer on my toxicity level, but I complied. He was like three times my size. I remember his overgrown mustache, cascading over his mouth like the lip of a wave, curling. "Grr. Get out of my bar." I think that's what he said. It's all a daze.

We were on Venice Beach, California. Why wouldn't I leave that money-sucking beer tit to sit on a sandy shore for free-ninety-nine? After all, I had just spent three thousand dollars producing my first short film. Free sounded great.

I moved my sunglasses, from the top of my head, to cover my eyes, as I watched the orange sun setting over the blue horizon. Its reflection off the ocean's surface reminded me of a time when life was simpler. I could lose myself in this memory.

The sound of the water receding from the shore. The faint scent of salt in the air. The cry of seagulls, circling above. Where could I have possibly gone in my mind? Maybe it doesn't matter. Moving on.

My memory is choppy. Please excuse my drunken prose.

The next thing I remember is lying prostrate on the beach. I wept, my face in the sand. I didn't know where my friends were. I didn't know why I was crying.

"Excuse me?"

I probably didn't hear it the first time.

"Excuse me, are you okay?"

I turned toward the voice. Above me, on the pier, I saw the silhouette of boy leaning against the railing. The sunlight disappeared behind him, leaving his face in shadow. Yet, I noticed a subtle glow around the shape of his head. Kind of like, a halo?

"I'm fine, thanks."

What else could I say? No, I'm not fine? I can't talk about it because there's nothing to discuss? I feel completely disoriented and I don't know who my friends are? Oh, now is a good time to explain that I'm bipolar. I cry for no reason sometimes. Or maybe I just don't know them.

I rolled over and reached into my pocket for my phone, and called her, Nikola Woolf, again.

Yeah, I'm aware that excessive calling or texting is not the best way to attract a woman. They hate that shit. But I was drunk, crying for no apparent reason, and I wanted to hear her voice.

Note that the difference between psychotic behavior and storybook romance is a thin line. If she loves you, you're Prince Charming. If she doesn't, you may as well be Norman Bates.

That, ladies, is why we're afraid to be romantic.

Well, I'm not.

The truth now.

Yes, yes, I am.

Then again, I've been called "psycho" more times than I'd like to admit.

Hmm. I probably should've kept that one in my pocket, huh?

Dear Honesty, you are killing me.

Moving on.

I asked, "Are you still coming? Because if you're not, just tell me."

Doubt and insecurity seeped through my pores with the depression of my lonely childhood. Oh, why did I have to play those stupid drinking games?

Because. I'm a lesbian, and that means I'm supposed to be one of the guys. The easiest way to earn respect amongst a group of young men is to drink those punks under the cliched table of their ego-induced manhoods. And I did. How could I possibly make a good first impression at this point?

"Yes," she replied. "I'm almost there. Okay?"

I exhaled. "Yeah. Okay."

"I'll see you soon."

"Okay.... bye."

It had been eight years of phone calls, texting, long periods of silence while either of us were in relationships. I remember nights when I fell asleep to the sound of her voice, like a lullaby, serenading my heart into near submission.

Nikola made promises I dared not believe. She was like the tooth fairy. It isn't real, is it? It's just something we believe in when we're dumb and naive. I wasn't either of those things. I think.

I was sure that Nikola had a collection of pretty girls, eating up her sweet talk like Halloween candy. Not me. I wanted her to know that I was worth more than that. If, indeed, she was a player, I hoped she would see that I was not among her shiny toys.

There are two types of females. There are the girls that you grow out of, and the women that you grow into. I would be the latter.

Despite my apprehensions, I was drawn to her, time after time. Then again, there was always something keeping us apart. It was like an eight-year game of phone tag, missed connections, and the repeated operator's message:

"I'm sorry, the person you are trying to reach is in a relationship. Please try again in eighteen to twenty-four months."

We had never met in person. Tonight would be the night. And my dumb ass was drunk.

I saw her name flashing on the screen of my phone. I picked myself up out of the sand and cleared my throat. "Hello?"

"Hey. Which pier are you at?" She asked.

The pier in California? I thought.

I strolled toward the concrete structure, stretching out toward the ocean. "There's more than one?"

"Are you wearing red?"

I looked down at my shirt. Oh shit. It's red.

I laughed.

Wait. That means she can see me.

She giggled. "I see you."

Really? That's not fair.

Then, she was standing in front of me.

I probably looked like shit because I'd been crying my eyes out. Not to mention my breath reeked like beer. She didn't seem to mind.

On the other hand, she looked like perfection.

Her bone structure was exquisite, defining her cheeks and jaw. Her almond-shaped eyes suggested some sweet sadness. Her light brown irises invited me to stare into them, to explore the mysteries they veiled. I somehow knew they had stories to tell, and I was intent to listen.

Every detail of her face was perfect. For each patch of skin, curve, and outline, I could see God sweating at the forehead, bent over, working tirelessly on, surely, their most perfect creature.

I stared a little longer than I should have.

It's not like I didn't know what she looked like. I knew she was beautiful on the outside, having drooled over her pictures long enough. But, physical beauty never impressed me much. I always wanted more. I was never quite sure what I was searching for, until this moment.

Love at first sight is the only real love. It transcends time, you see. This love has existed long before our conception, and will continue after we have returned to dust. Love is constant. There is no beginning or end.

I watched as she pushed a strand of hair behind her ear. "I just came from work."

I opened my arms, a silent invitation, and we embraced for the first time. But, the feeling was nothing new. It felt as if I had slept there, my head on her chest, many nights before, like an infant would rest on its mother's breast.

Nikola's energy was more than familiar. It reminded me of the person I was when I was born. The child I was, well, as a child. She felt like someone I had known all my life. Me.

We took a walk on the pier. I don't remember what was said. I kept my eyes on her, intent on her every breath. My heart felt each step she took toward the edge of that dock. For every creak and wave that crashed upon its stilts below, each speechless moment felt lighter, rendering my body weightless.

I turned my heart into a kite.

I noticed the curve of her bottom lip. It called out to me, like a ripe piece of fruit to a parched tongue. I contemplated a kiss. As I turned my gaze from her face, to the peeling paint on the iron railing, I was reminded that I would have to leave soon, back to Las Vegas, to my fiancé.

Stay in the moment, Kelly.

Okay.

So, I stared into her light brown eyes, boldly, as if knocking on the door to her innermost secret chambers. I spotted tiny freckles on her irises, admired the design, and felt connected to her Creator.

God, did you make this?

Nikola didn't shy from my gaze. On the contrary, she stared back, allowing the moment to unleash whatever forces were upon us now. Every cell in my body longed to be closer to her, and instinctively, I knew, the feeling was mutual.

CHAPTER 9

Nikola Woolf
Involuntary Travel

This need for comprehension is both the foundation and drive of this experiment. I have discovered the key sequence, successfully created two live models of the quantum human, but utterly failed to find solution to this seemingly simple question.

What is love?

Love is not matter, not elemental, not ether. Its effects are observed, measured, and predicted, yet definition as elusive, as my tender heart reclusive.

What is love?

Love is more than emotion. Nerve impulses are expended and neutralized. Yet love so irrationally remains, generating its own power and expansion, much like the nature of universe.

What is love?

Love is more than chemistry. Hormonal responses naturally build to more euphoric states, orgasmic bliss, yet this is merely love's effect.

Love is more than magnetics. The auric interaction between lovers, attraction, repulsion, electromagnetic compulsions, the aurora of her heart. These are vague descriptions of the nature of love, so far from definition.

I set out to discover truth, and here I sit, no longer human. I am without knowledge. The path I am on does not promise answer to my most desperate question.

I need new technology.

12 AUG 2022

I was sitting at my desk when it happened again. My physical awareness faded until I found myself in a dark void, in between places, or in two realities at once. It felt like darkness pressing in all around me, like I had been tossed into outer space, with no point of reference by which I might grip my own sanity.

I tried to reach for my sense of logic, but found myself increasingly lost and afraid. Instead, I embraced both my terror and absolute ignorance. Then, and only then, did I find myself on solid ground again. Still, I was unsure of my location.

It was some kind of palace. The setting sunlight, reflected off golden pillars, blinded my sight. I looked down to relieve my burning eyes, and noticed a mosaic of stones, lapis lazuli, turquoise, jade, and obsidian. My feet were barefoot on the cold tile. I stepped into a shadowy corner of the room, and whispered, "Where am I?"

A man walked pass me, and approached the sunlight. He appeared spectacular in a gown of golden threads. He dropped to one knee, and as he bowed his head, I saw her. The man said, "My queen."

The throne must have been at least twenty feet in height, made of gold, mahogany, lion skins, and tortoise shell. In it sat the queen, adorned with jewelry and makeup.

Her voice echoed throughout the room. "Where is my son?"

The man stood. "Your majesty, the Roman army is at the gate. Octavius is on his way, right now."

"I said, where is my son?"

The man tensed with hesitation. I felt my throat constricting. "Queen Cleopatra, please. We are going to die. Our numbers are small and we cannot hold the gate for long. Please speak to Octavius and ask him to spare us."

The next moment was suspended in the now singularity. Fear, rage, and hope seemed to dance around a surreal carrousel. All of the Multiverse was revolving around this moment. The queen's decision was like a pebble, tossed into the waters of infinite worlds.

Finally, the queen said, "Charmion, do you still consider me a friend?"

The man nodded. "Of course. Since we were children, you have been my best friend, Cleo. I love you. My queen, you have changed since."

"Do you mean, since Octavius murdered my husband, stole my son's birthright, and corrupted my soldiers? Yes, I have changed. Octavius is poised to destroy our sacred city, and you are asking me to bow before this filthy pig?"

Charmion cast his eyes to the floor. "My queen, I am begging you."

"It shall never happen."

I felt a storm brewing under Cleopatra's skin. Her ability to make a hurricane appear still, gave me a chill. "Where, Charmion, is my son?"

I heard a voice from across the hall, the sound of footsteps. A young man stepped into the sunlight. I noticed his jawline, wide and definite. It was identical to his father's.

In that moment, I had a flash of recollection. I saw the young man's birth, in a sacred hot spring. I caught a vision of his first steps, walking into the arms of his father.

I saw him, Julius Caesar, his face shape-shifted into that of... Kelly.

In this moment I downloaded a file, information of rich sensation, regarding Kelly and our past, the reasons we could not be together in this life. Or could we? More later.

I understood that this boy was my son.

The young man held his chin up. His eyes were honey in the setting sunlight. "I am here, Mother."

Confusion stole over me, but only for a moment. First Virginia, now Cleopatra? This was a past life regression, surely. No, I could not have been these historical figures. There was another explanation. There is.

The queen relaxed in her throne. I felt her exhale. Cleopatra's voice was soft, like the white rose petals from which Caesarion's first bed was made. "Caesarion, come." Her firstborn was her favorite.

The young man approached the throne. His heart longed to rush into his mother's arms and adorn her with hugs and kisses. Instead, he forced himself to stand still, like a man. Caesarion clenched his fists and flexed his chest, back, and arms. He had been training with the Roman soldiers, and he wanted his mother to see that he was a man. It was his time to come of age. He felt ready.

"Mother, I wish to sacrifice myself to Octavius."

Cleopatra chuckled, moving her head more freely now. "That shall never happen, Son."

"Please listen. I never wanted to be dictator of Rome. I do not care for what Caesar did or did not do. All I wanted was to be here in Alexandria with you. I never wanted it to go this far. I do not wish for more bloodshed on my behalf. I will go to Octavius and ask him to cease the war."

"Caesarion, my son."

"Please, Mother. You said that I was destined to be great. You told me to behave like royalty. I believe this is what a regent should do for his country. Mother, do you see, this is why I practiced the Latin tongue, and I studied the Roman religion, and the Roman law. Not because I wanted to be like Caesar, but because I am a Roman. If Rome would murder their own kind, as they did my father, then I would be honored to die for Egypt.

"Mother, let Octavius take me to Rome, let me be his prize. I do not care for appearances. I value truth. Send me, Prince of Egypt, please, I pray thee, my mother and queen. Let Alexandria be spared. Or we shall all be dead by morning."

I watched as Charmion held his tongue, and Cleopatra went inside herself.

Another decision was to be made. The queen could not stop her son, but she would never approve of this plan. Cleopatra's love for the people was murdered with her dear Julius. Caesarion was all that was left of him.

The queen had watched her son grow in appearance, more and more like Caesar, everyday. In armor, Caesarion might look identical to his father. Cleopatra thought of how the sight of Caesar in full battle dress might strike terror in the heart of Octavius.

Caesarion stood with his hands behind his back, waiting, with respect, for his mother's decision.

That's when a Roman soldier walked in. I knew who he was. I felt him move pass me, almost as if he had moved through me. He stood beside the throne. "My queen, the tomb is ready. The army is here, we must move quickly."

Cleopatra exhaled, turning her attention to the man. She ran her fingers through his dark curly lochs. "Marc, my love. I will be there soon." They kissed, and he walked out.

The queen waited another moment before speaking. "Caesarion, do you remember what your father taught you about warfare?"

The boy nodded. "Yes, Mother. Marc Antony has trained me as well."

Cleopatra leaned in and whispered. "Your father was the greatest warrior who ever lived. Rome is because of Caesar. The greatness that built Rome lives inside you. Go into my chambers, into my golden chest, and you will find your father's armor and sword. Listen, son.

"I want you to go to Octavius, but I do not want you to surrender. I want you to kill him. I want you to avenge your father's murder. Do this, for me?"

Caesarion shifted. He glanced at his feet. I felt his throat constrict, his heart grow heavy. He fought the urge to cry. He returned his eyes to the queen, pushing his emotions down below. "Yes, Mother. I will do this for you."

"I love you, my son."

Caesarion jumped into her arms, knowing they would never embrace again.

Ancient Egypt started fading from my reality, as my mind was wiped clean of memory. Some force of nature was pulling me out of that world, and into the next. It felt like blood draining from my veins. I grew drowsy, relaxed enough to allow the process. I had no choice but to surrender.

Then I was standing in a mission control station. I stood for a moment to let the vertigo pass.

In the center of the vessel, there was a holographic map of the Multiverse, countless blue and green marbles of life, infinite versions of Earth, against the dark matter of space.

There were electronic instruments there, all far more advanced than anything I had ever seen. I realized in that moment, that I had been summoned. But by whom?

"Hi." A young man stood, not ten feet away. He appeared to be a bionic human. He wore a robotic helmet, only half his face showing. His right arm was mechanical. His energy was friendly. "My name is Trayvon Johnson, but I have many names. You do, too."

I tried to press his mindspace, but found an electronic barrier. I wondered if it could be hacked. I stood a moment longer, unsure of myself. I had an eerie feeling about him, and could not define it. Finally, I gathered my courage. I went closer and offered my hand. "Nikola Woolf."

Trayvon, now towering above me, took it. "Dr. Woolf, it's a pleasure. You can't read my mind, and if you wanna survive your own ascension, let me help me. I mean, you. I wanna help you."

An interesting slip, I thought.

Trayvon held his robotic arm toward the corner of a room where a few chairs gathered around a coffee table. "Please sit, we got a lot to talk about."

He seemed like a child to me, a prodigy. I was interested in studying him.

I nodded. "Let's."

Trayvon sat and nervously brought his hands together on his knees. "I'm not really a prodigy, doctor. I'm just a lucky-ass kid. I'm the only human survivor of my world. I come from a timeline that stems off yours. I guess you could say I'm from your future, 2084 to be exact. But since time's not real, we have a chance to save humanity, not just in both our worlds, but in as many as 5.5 trillion.

"This station is in a pocket universe, a secret one. I created it after my Earth was destroyed. She's moved on to the sixth dimension, but those who were left behind, well, it was hell. This place, pocket headquarters, is my home now."

"When you say 'she,' you mean,"

"The life force of the planet. Gaia, I think, is her most popular name. When she left us, the rain became acidic, all vegetation died. The oceans died. All hope for us was lost. Democracy was overthrown and the president of the US became dictator, and commander in chief. Martial law was the only law.

"I was part of an underground resistance, but it was a major fail. In the end, the commander in chief abandoned ship and nuked the planet. It was kind of like the great flood, except, ain't nothin' growing back this time. I used the blast from the nuke to create, well, this."

It was not hard to believe that the extinction of humanity was a reality. I took a moment to observe before speaking. Trayvon reminded me of Caesarion.

Emotional memories of Caesarion and our life in Egypt surfaced.

I recalled that Caesarion was more partial to academics than to military life, while Caesar lived only for battle, and admired the well-read. Cleopatra carried both traits.

I recalled how it was far easier to love Caesarion than it was to love Caesar.

I told myself to come back to the present, to Trayvon.

I released the Egyptian memories, as my surroundings came into clear awareness, like a camera coming into focus.

The bionic boy watched me, also observing my visions. I came back to his energy, his story. The future space station hiding in a pocket universe.

"Trayvon," I said, "you're the only human survivor of your world. You've created a pocket universe with advanced technology. You attribute all this to luck. I find that fascinating, Trayvon. You summoned me here, didn't you? How and why?"

Trayvon lifted his hand and scratched his helmet, then chuckled. "Ah, I'm not used to this thing. Yeah, I've been monitoring the Multiverse for humans crossing the threshold into the fifth dimension. The helmet supports my brain development, thanks to your book, the Love Papers, I was able to build robotic body parts before reaching the threshold. I know you're still writing it. Trust me, it'll change everything. I summoned you using an angelic frequency, which cannot be picked up by the dark ones.

"Long story short, doctor, my world was destroyed by an aggressive alien race. The dark ones are slave masters and they run the world in trillions of universes. Humans are like cattle to them, and our species is in a state of arrested development. Kinda like how people used to tie a baby cow down so it couldn't move? Then eat it? That's basically what humanity is, a chained child, awaiting slaughter. Karma is kinda crazy, huh?" Trayvon chucked. "Anyway, anyone who crosses the threshold into the fifth dimension is hunted down and killed. So, your welcome. Now you know your life is in danger. And, welcome to the adolescence of human kind."

I knew this. His words resonated deep inside me. That otherworldly terror, it was always real. "Tell me more about these dark ones."

Trayvon stared down for a moment. His energy shifted as I felt fear weigh down on his shoulders, settling deep within his body. He took a deep breath. "Some call them aliens, but the angels are ET, too. Some call them demons. But I don't think it's black and white like that. Maybe it is." He shrugged. "I don't know. What I do know is that there's a dark lord named Psyfon. He works for the slavemasters, and he's got a headhunter after us. A powerful one, his name is Condor. But there's something more. It's like I'm missing information. Something doesn't make sense." He stared away, his stress levels increasing.

For whatever reason, fear escaped me. The angels were certainly not what Christianity made them out to be. They had good intentions, sure, but I did not believe in righteousness. Demons, or, the bipolar opposite of angels, of course they would have dark intentions. These are natural conditions of duality. Creation and destruction. Power and oppression. The answer was no answer, and yet, there was another question in his heart.

I said, "Perhaps it's not time to know. Are you safe here?"

Trayvon nodded. "For now. I need a power source to sustain the shields. Without the barrier, this pocket would fade into the radioactive zone surrounding what used to be planet Earth.

"Don't get me wrong, Doc, I'm glad you ain't afraid. But you haven't seen them destroy everything you love. They consume entire worlds, they have infinite at their disposal. This is a bad-guy buffet, and human is on the menu. The angels, they just stand by like medics. They ain't saving us. We have to save humanity, but before this goes one step further, you should know.

I interrupted. "Trayvon, you said you read the Love Papers? How did it help you, exactly?"

The energy shifted as we both asked ourselves why I rejected the information. Whatever he was about to tell me was not for me to know. Not yet, at least.

I took a deep breath as the new vibration settled between us.

Trayvon leaned forward, his elbows on the table, and rested his chin in his hands. "I shouldn't have said that, no. It ain't really safe to tell people their future."

I took a deep breath and chose my words carefully. "You mentioned the Love Papers, I think, for a reason. I need to make a breakthrough. I need to cure myself. I need new technology. Please, tell me what you read."

Trayvon looked up at me, surprised. "Cure yourself of love? But, doctor, love is medicine. Kelly Perez is your true partner for all eternity, and Doctor, we need her.

"You reject Kelly because you reject yourself. She reflects everything you hate about yourself. That's why you can't stand her, and yet you can't stop feeling her inside you. She's you, doctor.

"It's not possible to love another if you don't love yourself. That's a general rule, but for twin flames, it's scientific law."

He leaned forward, looked into my eyes. "You and Kelly Perez are in a state of quantum entanglement. This can be measured, tested, predicted. The summary, doctor, the conclusion of it all, well, it's beyond anything that can be written or spoken. You gotta feel it, experience it. Take the plunge, doc. That means putting your heart on the line. I'm sure that's what you needed to hear to take your experiment to the next level."

There was a moment of silence as I contemplated my immediate future. Why could I not see it as Mr. Johnson sees his?

"Doctor," he went on. "You are Virginia Woolf and Cleopatra. You'll come across other versions of you as your consciousness peaks. The famous lifetimes come up first 'cause you're already partly aware of them." Trayvon waved his hand in a particular way. I took it for an electronic command.

He went on. "Don't let your ego take you for a ride, though. Power is dangerous, as you already learned. The Tower of Babel was brought down by its own pride. Humility, Dr. Woolf, is what keeps us sane."

A droid, far more advanced than the robots in my world, approached us. If it were not for its blank stare, it would have passed for a human. It set a bottle and two glasses down.

Trayvon picked up the liquor and poured. "Thank you, Rosie." He slid one glass toward me as the droid left us. "This is an elixir containing a biogenetic supplement. Can you guess what it's for?"

I paused a moment, feeling the liquid in my hands. I could request the information from my mind, or, I could intuit the feeling in the glass. I chose the feeling.

I felt tiny conscious beings, swimming about. They tickled my palm, joyful in nature, as they were programmed to be. Their purpose, I felt, was to feed my blood cells the energy needed to initiate rapid mitosis. For, I feared, I may die soon.

Trayvon chucked, "Dropping blood is normal at first. The bionic cells will multiply as the crystalline alchemizes to carbon again. There's a trigger in the protein sequence."

As I drank the concoction, I learned its recipe. I would recreate it in the lab.

I folded my hands and took a good look at my companion. He still had baby fat, light facial hair. I guessed seventeen. His wisdom was ancient. I said, "Tell me who you are, your famous lifetimes."

Trayvon's smile widened. He laughed. "Aw, really. It's kind of embarrassing."

I nodded, as I extracted the information from his auric field. "Malcom X. Chief Geronimo." Then, suddenly, the channel was disconnected.

"Come on, that's enough." Trayvon shook his head, he hugged his knees to his chest for a moment. "Look, everything I have ever done was based on stupidity and luck."

"You mean bravery and trust."

"I'm not a genius."

"You've won me over, Trayvon. You remind of my son." There was a long moment of silence as I lost myself in the memory of Caesarion. I didn't realize how much I yearned for a child, more specifically, for him.

I felt the gravity of Cleopatra's choice come down on my chest. I heard the screams of her people, the rumbling of her city. The grief, the remorse, the weight of a thousand worlds pressed against the outside of my tomb.

I died a corrupt politician. I was the most powerful woman in the world, and I wasted it all on a false self of godhood. Because of me, thousands died. I failed as queen. I failed as Cleopatra.

Curse the golden statue, Julius. You led me down a dark path.

Then, I saw him lying there, Marc Antony, in bloody battle dress, rushed upon his own sword, at my feet. The man I married took his life because I asked him to? No, I told him to.

The vision ended, and I looked up at my companion, the bionic boy.

Trayvon leaned in closer, blinked, and said. "You're fading. Condor is hunting us, you need to-"

Then I was sitting in the passenger seat of a sedan. It was nighttime, and the car was in motion, reckless driving. Kelly was in the drivers seat. She appeared much younger, her mid-twenties, I guessed.

The car was littered with water bottles, fast food packages, gym clothes, and trash. I remembered this car. This must have been fifteen years into the past, before we had met in person. Kelly was not so sloppy anymore.

She glanced at my direction.

"Look, Nikola, I know that I'm crazy. But it really feels like you're sitting here in my car with me. I don't care what it looks like to anyone else. I may as well embrace the crazy, right?"

Kelly seemed to look deep into my eyes, then threw a glance at the road, swerving away from the curb. "See, it's like you're invisible." She laughed. "I love being psychotic because I can talk to invisible people in my car.

"Anyways babe, I feel bad for not calling you back or texting you. I know that's what you want from me right now. But it's just that you keep spitting game at me, and that's not gonna work, boo. Please just tell me something real. I want to know how you really feel, like, show me your heart."

I let the silence set in for a moment, as I watched Kelly run her fingers through her short, boyish hair. Her eyes moved from the rearview mirror, to the side views, to the road, then back to me. I realized that I liked watching her when she thought she was alone.

I said, "Kelly, it's real. I'm here in the car with you."

Kelly nodded. "Yeah, I know. I'm psychotic. If you knew I was talking to you in my head, you would probably call me psycho and never speak to me again."

"You have a gift, Kel. Your exes called you psycho, and maybe you've done some unhealthy things, but that's not who you are. You can communicate with unseen entities. That's brilliant."

Kelly reached into a paper bag in the center console for a french fry. Her mouth half full, she said, "Well, thanks. That means a lot coming from a figment of my imagination." She laughed. "See, why can't we have conversations like this?"

I recognized the city of Las Vegas, the neon lights of Fremont Street.

Kelly ran a red light, as a car swerved to miss us. "Listen, Nikola. You're so hot, you probably get every woman you go after. The only reason you want me is because you can't have me. But when you're done being a player, let me know. Until then, we will have imaginary conversations in my car."

It was no use trying to argue. She was convinced of her insanity, and by definition, she really was psychotic.

I asked. "So, you were attracted to me then? I mean, you are?"

"Hell yeah," Kelly glanced at me. "I think about you when I masturbate."

"Really?" I was surprised to learn that this is the kind of information I desired.

She chuckled. "Yeah, I have a pretty intense sex drive, and you take me there. It's too bad you think you're a player."

"What if I told you I'm not a player?"

Kelly shoved another fry in her mouth. "I would call you *una mentirosa.* You lie."

I scoffed, leaned back into my seat, arms crossed. "The truth finally comes out. You really don't trust me."

"Nope. You lie about your age, your relationship status, what else? Everything you say is game. Don't get me wrong, I like it. But if you want something real with me, you gotta get real with me."

Kelly's phone went off, and I watched as she reached into her pocket. "Hey, what's up? ...No dude, just talking to my imaginary friend.... Nope, we broke up on Wednesday.... because fuck her, that's why. The point is I'm single until next week.... Oh, it's what's her face's birthday, that one chic I made out with at the bar that one night.... yep, her, well, her birthday is next weekend. I'm gonna take her out and make her my new girlfriend. But that gives us one whole weekend, bro.... Ew, that's my ex, but go ahead. She's all yours, dawg.... Yeah, I'm sure.... Girlbar, yeah, I'm down.... Okay, late."

Kelly tossed her phone through my lap and shoved another fry into her mouth.

"And you call me a player."

Kelly glanced over again. "Oh, Niko. The difference between you and me, is that you lie to people, you hide things. That's called playing. But everyone I fuck with, they know what's up, and I'm faithful."

"Excuse me? I'm faithful, too. Look, if I'm not in a relationship with that person, I don't owe them anything, and furthermore,"

"The point is, you lie and hide shit, that's called being a player. But when you're straight up and give people the truth they deserve, and they still wanna stick around," Kelly popped her collar. "That's called big pimpin, Mami. Feel free to take notes."

I scoffed. "Wow, you're conceited."

Kelly looked into my eyes again. "Yeah, I know. My ego is all I have. The truth is I'm psychotic, I hate myself, and no one else loves me either. That doesn't exactly attract a whole lot of chics. You feel me? What about you, Niko? What's your truth?"

Then, I was being yanked out that world, violently, it seemed.

I woke up at my desk, groggy and confused, to the sound of Lisa's thoughts. She stood above me, a manuscript in hand.

She's love sick. That's the answer. My best friend is love sick and that's why she's losing her shit.

As I came to, I noticed the clothes I was wearing, trying to remember when I had put them on. I wondered how long I had been out for this time. I reached for my glasses, but before I brought them to my eyes, I realized that my vision was perfect.

"Hey, best friend." Lisa pulled a chair up beside mine. She flashed a fake smile, angry and sarcastic. "Remember when I told you I would send out an inquiry for love stories? Now I understand what you meant when you said, 'the story is true.'" Lisa dropped the manuscript on my desk. The title page read:

THE LOVE PAGES
by Kelly Perez

Lisa said, "But how did you know she was writing it? Don't answer that. I think her philosophies align with yours. You know, your idea of soulmates. Or, dare I say, twin flames? Coincidence? She named her story 'the Love Pages.' That's intense, don't you think? But the coolest part about it. There's this character named Nadia Roof. I think I can convince her to change it to Nikola Woolf. It just has a better ring to it. What do you think?"

Vertigo took hold of me, as the urge to vomit crept into my chest. Lisa's words had registered but I had not the energy to reply. I let my head fall onto my desk. I felt a sharp pain in my heart, twisting my guts. Then everything went black, again.

I regained consciousness in Lab one, lying on the exam table. I heard the voices of Luke and Lisa. I decided to eavesdrop for a moment.

Luke tried to keep his volume low. "You might think that she has this all under control, but I'm telling you. Whatever she's doing is dangerous. I will not take the fall for any illegal, not to mention, immoral acts. Talk some sense into her, because once I leave the institute, there will be no one to cover her tracks."

There was a moment of silence before Lisa spoke. "You know what, Skywalker? If you're that concerned about your career, don't let the door hit you. I'm worried about her life."

"I am, too."

I heard Luke walk out, and felt Lisa shift her attention to me. "If you don't wake up and get your shit together, bestie, I will contact Kel..."

The next thing I knew, I was standing in a dark cell made of rock and iron. Torches along the walls cast moving shadows everywhere. Moonlight shone in through a window, onto a hooded figure, huddled in the corner. The stench of urine and vomit came to my awareness. Outside the iron cell, I noticed the guard fast asleep, sitting upright in a chair.

The prisoner cast off its hood, and gazed at me. "Guardian angel, you have come, at last."

I stared in astonishment. It was Kelly. Except that her hair was blond, her skin light, and her eyes blue. Otherwise, it was an identical match.

The prisoner wore a tattered and bloodstained cloak. The agony in her heart, the confusion, the fear, they invaded my reality like an ominous mist on a dreadful morning.

Kelly got down on both knees, and pressed her forehead to the floor. She returned her gaze to me. "Guardian angel, I am Joan d'Arc, knight of

France, and messenger of the holy Christ. I have kept my sacred vows and confessed my sins. Please, sweet angel, they are going to kill me if I do not give false testimony." Joan turned toward the sleeping guard.

When she faced me, her blue eyes glistened with tears. Her lips trembled as she spoke. "Why do they hate me? The king has abandoned me. My only desire was to serve the holy Christ, the same God they also serve. I do not understand. Please, I pray thee, help?"

I was struck by her innocence. Did Joan not understand that their love was not real? That she was only a pawn to her government? That people use each other everyday?

I recalled the story of Joan d'Arc, and wondered how much truth was preserved by history. I accessed a stream of information.

It was during the Hundred Years War between France and England.

After serving the king of France as a messenger of god, and a fierce warrior, she was taken by French traitors, handed over to the enemies. There in English custody, the Catholic Church accused Joan of heresy, murdered her, and then made her a saint. Joan was burned alive at the stake.

I caught a vision of her body engulfed in flames. It struck my heart and took my breath.

I felt a surge of rage energize my nervous system. My body was exploding with heat, as I heard Joan's voice, screaming, "Jesus," again and again.

Torture by fire. Hell on earth, by authority of religion. This was a system designed to lure innocence, monopolize absolution, and control populations.

The moment passed as I grounded myself in the prison cell. My body was not on fire. This was Joan's imminent future. It would be unwise to change this fate. Or would it?

I recalled how Kelly helped Virginia. I would help Joan.

I knelt before her and took her into my arms. Joan rushed into my embrace, like a child, and broke down into a bawl. In that moment, my carbon body materialized, and I found that I was flesh and blood. Warm tears streamed down my face, in silence. I don't remember the last time I allowed myself to cry. I didn't think I could be this strong, but for her, I would.

I leaned back onto the stone wall. Joan fell asleep in my arms.

If I wanted to change her fate, I could.

Wait. Why could Joan see and touch me now, but Kelly, in our world, could only hear? What was causing the crystalline cells to transmute back to carbon?

Suddenly, the entire prison was blinding white. I gave my eyes a moment to adjust as the being came into view. It was my guardian angel.

Our guardian angel?

They looked into my eyes and spoke telepathically. *Well done, Nikola. You are evolving nicely, right on schedule.*

I glared up at the angel. *Isn't it your job to protect us?*

The angel folded its great wings, and knelt down before me. Their face glowed a golden hue, a symmetrically perfect statue. Their white and yellow eyes shone brilliant with intelligence and peace.

Yes. I am here to protect you both. However, I cannot save you from your own will. Joan chose this path everyday of her life. If she wishes, she could appease the priest to spare herself. Joan is willing to die for her mission. It was never about saving France. It was to warn humanity of the dark side of religion.

She is destined to die, then?

It is her choice, Nikola. She is accustomed to suffering, but this is not permanent.

You've been manipulating her sickness for some divine cause?

Nikola, please understand. Joan d'Arc is not sick. She is a sovereign soul. Joan is a mighty warrior, and this is a warrior's path. When Joan chooses to die for her honor, because she will, you may help guide the soul out of the body with minimal suffering.

The angel stood. *You will take her to her medicine father, a middle realm of the Apache land. Take her to Geronimo. You will learn much upon arriving. You are exhausted, Nikola. Save your questions. Rest now.*

I wanted to argue with the angel, but I could not resist sleep. I closed my eyes. After a few moments, taken by curiosity, I took a peek.

We were surrounded by glowing giants. Their light was like a hot, relaxing bath. I slept.

ABOUT THE AUTHOR

Akasha Torres grew up on the island of Oahu, in the Kingdom of Hawaii. They have been writing poetry, journaling, and traveling a spiritual path since childhood.

Akasha's friends call them Aka.

After graduating from Waipahu High School in 1999, Torres served in the active duty Air Force and was discharged honorably. In 2006, they moved to Las Vegas, NV and worked in the construction industry before earning an associates degree in Creative Writing from College of Southern Nevada.

They published a memoir in 2007 and a novel in 2012. Both titles are currently out of print.

Aka also explored filmmaking and acting. In 2013 Torres wrote, produced, and starred in a short film entitled *The Tell-Tale Heart*, a modern adaptation of Edgar Allan Poe's classic short story. That same year, Torres produced a teaser trailer for her debut novel, with the intention of producing a feature film.

In 2013-2014 Aka co-wrote, co-produced, and co-starred in two stage plays, "Only Fools" and "The Beloved," with Logan Writes.

In 2014, Torres played a featured background role in Tim Story's *Think Like a Man Too*.

Aka met their Twin Flame while filming in Hollywood and moved to Los Angeles only two months later.

In 2016, Torres enrolled at LA Film School and met Professor Houston Howard, the leading Hollywood expert on transmedia (he literally wrote the book).

While studying transmedia, Aka decided to give up filmmaking to design *the Multiverse*; a transmedia mega-story.

Torres is now the owner of Mercury Direct, a Portland-based indie imprint. They look forward to bringing together a team of indie artists to produce graphic novels, video games, and volumes of thrilling fiction and big-budget screenplays.

Aka was conditioned into Christianity during childhood, and became a Christian minister in 2008. They taught Sunday School lessons and occasionally gave sermons under Reverend Wilfred Moore at Abundant Peace Christian Church, UCC.

Torres said, "I will always cherish my relationship with Christ. However, Christianity excludes entire groups of people from the Round Table. That's not justice. I had to keep searching."

Torres explored Hinduism, Buddhism, and Paganism. In 2016, they answered the call to Shamanism. Aka is studying at Lightsong School of Shamanic Studies, an accredited mystery school.

Aka says, "Spirit tells me what to write. With Shamanic practice, I may ask a historical figure or diety, 'do you have a message for humanity?' and most of the time, they have something to say."

Aka is earning another degree in Creative Writing.

Akasha Torres is passionate about expanding the collective consciousness through story.